PANDORA'S STOWAWAY

and the double twist!

Dixie Dean

Cover design copyright: Polly Moseley MBA

With thanks to:
Polly Moseley, for her wizardry with the paint brush;
Steve Bullman, for his kindly Kindle expertise;
The children at No; 13, for their wise counsel;
Millie, for egging me on;
Liza and Peter, at Pandrillas.org, for their inspiration.

And for all those who care

CHAPTER 1

Pandora chugged out from her home port on the east coast of Africa into the calmest of calm seas on a journey the likes of which she had never undertaken before.

Pandora was an old paddle steamship who had been crossing the oceans of the world for many years carrying all sorts of useful things, such as cotton, tea, coffee, barley, spices, pins, buttons… I could go on, but I think you get the picture. She had been very busy in her lifetime.

But for quite some years now, she had been in what could only be called forced retirement, moored at the quayside. She had run out of her usefulness. Nowadays, bigger, more modern freighters had taken her place.

But just today, out of the blue, along the quay came a man who gleefully announced: "A-Ha! Just as I was hoping. This old crate is still sitting here. She'll do. A bit rusty, but she must have enough 'go' left in her for one more trip."

He was dressed as if for the jungle, in ragged shorts and an olive brown shirt with leather patches on the shoulders. On his feet were heavy boots which seemed to make him waddle rather than walk; unless his rather generous belly had something to do with it. His face seemed to be up-side-down, with no hair at the top but lots at the bottom. Of course, it didn't take rocket science to realize that he was bald and had a large beard. A beard which made him look quite angry, with long wiry whiskers sprouting in all directions. It wasn't your usual sailor's beard.

As he wandered off, he turned round to give Pandora a final look and said with a self-satisfied glint in his eye, "Yes, indeed, just what I need for my 'special' cargo. There's one thing missing, though."

All too soon, Pandora's creaky old crane was being put to work. It was quite mystifying to see what was coming aboard in her loading nets. There were bananas and berries and nuts going down into her storage hold; piles of leaves, too big to be tea leaves. You wouldn't get these into a pot! And they were still attached to branches. Big bunches of grass and hay came on as well. There was nothing that could really be called 'special', as the man had mentioned. Different, perhaps. But 'special'?

He brought quite a few personal bags and cases with him, some of which were rather bulky and made him struggle. The most notable addition to his luggage, and probably the 'one thing missing' was a satellite dish. If Pandora had ever had one, she didn't appear to have one now. Perhaps someone had 'relieved' her of it since she'd been inactive for so long. For years all ocean going ships have been rigged out with them to help with communications and navigation.

The new captain took great care positioning it on the big flag pole at her back, or in sea-going terms, at her stern.

After fixing the dish securely with bolts, he strode up and down Pandora, occasionally stamping on her decking as if testing it's strength. "Seems sound enough," he muttered. Then, patting his ample belly, he declared: "Right! Time to go and get my cargo," adding curiously, "Softly, softly, catchee monkey!"

He gave a celebratory tug on the cord that was supposed to make Pandora toot, but nothing came out. Her toot hadn't been used for a very long time.

"We'll have to get that fixed!" the captain retorted. "Can't go to sea without a decent toot!" But then he thought about it. "Hey ho, no matter. As long as her engine holds out for the journey, who gives a hoot if she can't toot?" And realising he had almost cracked a joke, he went off to round up his 'special' cargo.

As he waddled down the quay, he stopped for a moment to watch some cranes loading another boat. Numerous heavy metal boxes marked 'RR World Tour' were going aboard. He smiled to himself. 'No heavy boxes for me,' he mused, 'and no world tour, thank you very much!'

Also watching the boxes being loaded was a furry creature hidden in the bushes of an overgrown embankment at the end of the quay. For anyone who could have got a closer look at him, he might have seemed to be having a problem. And they would have been correct. 'Can't stay here much longer,' he was telling himself, frowning deeply. 'Gotta make my mind up one way or another real fast.' As luck would have it, something was soon to happen that made making up his mind that much easier. And real fast!

The man calling himself 'Captain'

CHAPTER 2

As the last RR box was about to join the others, our furry friend spotted the captain coming back along the quay. He was now carrying a flag which he held high. Following him, in a long line, were dozens and dozens of happy looking ANIMALS! 'Now, what's all this?' he asked himself. 'Very interesting!'

It seemed the captain had made a rapid change of clothes, for now he was wearing a white suit that was clearly a little small for him. It needed a press, too, looking as though it had just come out of a suitcase.

The animals tripped merrily along until the first ones reached Pandora's gang plank.

The captain went aboard first, still waving the flag, which had suddenly caught the furry creature's eye. Written on it in bold letters was; 'SIGHT-SEEING CRUISE TO EUROPE'.

He read it again and again to be sure he wasn't seeing things. 'This must be my lucky day,' he told himself. 'Europe! Now you're talking!'

The captain had made it to the top of the gangplank. "Come along, come along, everyone," he encouraged the animals with a broad grin as they climbed aboard in single file. As they passed him, he counted them carefully and noted down who was who. "Settle yourselves in as quickly as you can so that we can start our adventure without delay. There's more room upstairs than downstairs, but just as you please." Rather, above decks or below decks, it should have been.

"What a beautiful old steamship!" the animals were agreeing as they filed aboard.

"What a brilliant way to start a holiday!"

"It's so nice up here in the open. Let's sleep on deck!"

On they came, big ones and little ones. There were all sorts, all mixed up. And they were cheerfully speaking about going on holiday; Venice, Rome, Athens, even the Pyramids was being mentioned.

Little dik-diks came on, then larger antelopes; monkeys, chimpanzees and mandrills, some of these being very colourful - at both ends! There were zebras, rabbits, bush-babies, shrews; warthogs, aardvarks, pangolins, meerkats (or were they mongooses) - quite a few of them, whichever they were.

Trundling up came 3 elephants (two grown ups and one baby) who had to duck like the giraffes following them before they could find an open space to settle free of over-hanging ropes and things. After them came two baby hippopotamuses, seemingly without any parents, and just one rhinoceros, who didn't look anything like as happy as all the others.

Our furry friend had been watching closely, wondering how he might slip aboard without being noticed. He took his chance when he saw a group of hyraxes. He was a bit bigger than a hyrax, but he thought he might pass as one. The captain didn't appear to be at all fussy about who was coming onto Pandora, so he slotted nonchalantly in behind the largest hyrax and hoped to become just another 'tick' on the captain's entry list. This happened to be a mother hyrax, merrily hurrying her young daughter along.

"Off we go," she was saying.

"Why?" came the answer from the little hyrax.

"Because we're going on holiday."

"Why?"

"To see some wonderful sights."

"Why?"

"Because it will make us more knowledgeable."

"Why?"

To answer this, Mrs. Hyrax, Hyacinth was her name, took out a red berry and waved it at her child. "Would you like one of these?"

The answer to this was a big smile and a nod and the 'why's' stopped immediately.

This timely distraction had helped make good cover for our pretend hyrax as he skipped past the captain. But to make doubly sure he could safely relax, he immediately sought a spot where he could stowaway at least until they left port. He made sure he wasn't being watched, which wasn't too difficult with all the excitement of boarding going on, and slid discreetly under the tarpaulin covering one of Pandora's four lifeboats. 'Yep,' he congratulated himself as he settled down. 'Definitely my lucky day!'

After the hyraxes came a line of bonobos, who could easily be mistaken for chimpanzees but for their rather pink lips and longer hair that had a parting in the middle. Their leader ('Bono' was printed in big letters on his T-shirt) was extremely muscular. He was going through a rigorous routine of arm exercises as he jogged aboard. "Hup, one, two, stretch! Hup, one, two, stretch!" he called out to a line of youngsters to keep them in time as they followed him up the gangplank, flinging their arms to the side on the command of 'stretch' as if swatting flies. Bonobos were actually the very closest of cousins to human beings.

Everyone was spilling onto the deck so speedily that Pandora was soon fully loaded.

"That looks like everyone's aboard," the captain announced, slamming the railing gate shut. "Gangplank away! Cast off the lines, we are all set to go!"

Because they had long fingers, the monkeys and the chimpanzees were given the job of untying the ropes holding Pandora to the quayside. After that was done, the only thing left was to raise the anchor.

Mr. Elephant did this, being very strong. He took the chain in his trunk and in no time the anchor was up out of the water.

By now, Pandora's engines had warmed up. She gave a cough and a splutter as the captain shouted "Full speed ahead!"

Very slowly, but surely, as her paddles began to heave and turn for the first time in years. she began to move away from the quayside.

Fishing boats, ocean liners, oil tankers and a whole load of other ships and boats gave toots of farewell to Pandora as she huffed and puffed her way slowly out to the open sea.

What a send off!

Flags waved and fluttered long goodbye's. But soon they had been left behind as she made her way out into the ocean, chugging toward distant Europe.

Or so the animals thought!

Christopher at the wheel

CHAPTER 3

Pandora plodded on all that afternoon and through the night. By the next morning, she was a long way from her home port even though her old engines couldn't raise much speed. It would take a while to get her joints and pistons working smoothly again.

The animal who had been given the job of keeping Pandora on the right course was Christopher, a colobus monkey. Being such balmy weather, he had been up all night steering from the open helm. Having been strictly instructed by the captain, he had been keeping Pandora pointing in a set direction all the time.

"How's it going?" asked a deep voice as the sun rose in the East, "You must be feeling a little tired?" It was coming from Mr. Elephant. Mrs. Elephant and baby elephant were at his side.

"I am a bit, I must confess," Christopher replied. "But it was a lovely calm night. And now we're well and truly on holiday!"

He was such a jolly looking monkey, with a cheeky grin and a lovely crop of red hair. He had a twin brother, Colin, who preferred to be known as Archimedes after the great mathematician and scientist of that name. This was because Colin (please call me Archimedes) believed himself to be quite a good scientist himself. And it was sort of true. He loved to delve into things and work them out. Right now, he was probably somewhere on the boat trying to work out how many rivets Pandora had in her hull, or hanging a plumb weight over the side to see how deep the ocean was. Things like that really interested him.

Although Christopher had no interest in his brother's fascination for things scientific, what they did in common was a similar crop of red hair.

Now looking at one to the other of the family of elephants, something didn't seem quite right to Christopher. "Hmm. How peculiar," he remarked, not meaning to be impolite by staring so much, but not being able to stop himself all the same. Perhaps it was understandable, for all three elephants had differently shaped heads.

Mrs. Elephant had two little domes, more like 'bumps' on hers, Mr. Elephant had a sort of cone on his, and baby elephant was different to them both. That wasn't all, for Mr. Elephant's ears were far larger than Mrs. Elephant's. At least twice as large!

"I know what you're thinking," Mr. Elephant said graciously, noticing Christopher's interest in the dome on his head. "Mrs. Elephant is from Asia, you see. That's why she's got two 'bumps' on her head, not because she banged it coming aboard. I'm from Africa where we elephants have just one, sort of, dome on ours."

Mrs. Elephant went on to explain. "I came to Africa with my parents when I was small. I believe things weren't going too well for elephants there at the time. These days, mind you, things in Africa don't seem any better..."

Mr. Elephant cut her off. "Never mind all that, dear. Let's just enjoy this holiday while we can. Let's not complicate things."

Looking at baby elephant, Ella, was her name, Christopher was thinking, 'Yes, things are complicated enough."

Ella had just one 'bump', on the left side of her head, one large African ear on her right side, and a smaller Asian ear on her left.

Other animals had woken and heard what was being said. They gathered round to have a closer look at the elephants. There were 'oohs' and 'aahs', but cutting through them was a squeaky voice asking: 'Why?'

It was baby hyrax again, whose nickname was Nosy, not only for obvious reasons, but because, like her parents, she had rather a long nose for her size. Hyraxes were in fact distant relatives of Elephants, even having two long teeth like small 'tusks', if you looked closely enough.

Because Harry, Nosy's dad, didn't really know the answer to the elephants' ears and bumps situation, he produced one of the red berries he always carried for such moments. Nosy readily grabbed it, putting an end to her nosiness for the time being. "These work like magic with Nosy, as you can see," Harry said, holding up one of the red berries. "They have one of those very funny long names, but are better known as 'miracle berries', because they make bitter food taste sweet. True! Just try one when you chew on your next slice of lime."

With that nugget of interesting information to think about, the animals dispersed to enjoy their first full day on holiday.

CHAPTER 4

As the days passed, the animals were more or less left to their own devices. Apart from mealtimes, the captain only came out of his cabin to fiddle with the satellite dish, or to make sure that whoever was at the steering wheel had Pandora pointing in exactly the right direction, which always had to be on the same compass line. Not only because a straight line was the quickest way, they were told, to where they were going, but more importantly, as far as he was concerned, because the satellite signal to his computer would be lost if they strayed off that line. And he needed that satellite signal to bring his mission to fruition!

But at mealtimes, he was always in attendance to count and note the animals. On more than one occasion he would ask, "Is everyone here? Seems to be one missing." As far as the animals were concerned, they were all there. No-one was going to miss out on meals.

But the captain was absolutely correct, of course. A certain furry creature was never present.

It soon became clear that another reason he was always in attendance at meal times was to make sure no-one ate too much. "The stocks must last!" he would grumble. "If you're still hungry, suck on a slice of lime, with or without one of those miracle berries. Don't want you getting ill."

Sailors used to eat a lot of limes. It was full of Vitamin C and helped stop them getting a disease called scurvy. Some sailors had even been called 'limeys' in the old days.

There was a way, however, the captain stressed one evening, that more food could be made available. But only to those animals who could entertain him with some spectacular tricks or circus acts.

None of the animals gave much thought to that idea, though. This was something new. They were supposed to be on holiday, after all.

'Why would he be wanting circus acts?' Archimedes was wondering. And another thing that he had been wondering about was the captain saying that Pandora had to be kept on a straight line to get to where they were going. Having an interest in maps and countries, Archimedes knew full well they would have to make quite a few twists and turns before they got to Europe. The Red Sea and Suez Canal were in the way!

"Oh, well," he thought. Perhaps this man calling himself captain had arranged to restock somewhere on the way. No point worrying about it so early in their holiday.

They all seemed to be having a pleasant enough time relaxing and getting to know each other. Some of the younger ones had started playing games like hunt the miracle berry and hide and seek. Pandora had plenty of nooks and crannies around her decks to keep them occupied for hours. A favourite place to hide was in the lifeboats. There were four of them, but snoring always seemed to be coming from one of them, so they were told not to play near that one in case it disturbed whoever was having a good night's sleep; or good day's sleep, more appropriately. It seemed to go on non-stop, night and day.

Bono had taken to keeping his troupe of bonobos active by doing circuits of Pandora's upper deck, with brief interludes of running and stretching on the spot. "Hup, one, two, stretch! Hup, one, two, stretch!" Some of the chimps and monkeys joined in occasionally, but would sneak off when they'd had enough to do more leisurely things, like resting.

The large meerkat family liked to look out to sea. Mercedes and Merlin, the parents, would take it in turns to stand at the bow scanning the horizon for potential hazards.

"You look that way and I'll look this," Mercedes would boss Merlin, and would often add: "And keep your eye on the kids. Don't want them running off getting into trouble! Have you counted them lately?"

Merlin always had. "They're all here. Lined up behind you." But he counted them again just to be sure. The youngsters were happily copying their mother, not really knowing what they were supposed to be looking for. There didn't seem to be a lot to see out to sea, apart from the sea itself.

But what they did see on occasion were dolphins bobbing in and out of the water alongside Pandora with big smiles on their faces. They were having a great time playing in the bow-waves which amused the meerkats no end.

On other occasions, had they turned their glances to behind them and watched carefully, they might have been lucky enough to catch sight of some water spouts and big tails waving. One school of blue whales in particular would sometimes follow ships on the lookout for any waste being thrown overboard. They were constantly going up and down the coast pushing ashore the piles of plastic rubbish that somehow ends up in the ocean, a lot of it coming from ships and fishermen who should know better.

After a while, the dolphins waved goodbye and went off to play somewhere else and the meerkats' attention was directed to something happening on deck.

Two very nice looking antelopes seemed to be learning to dance. They were clip clopping up and down with their heads nuzzling so closely it was a wonder their rather spectacular horns didn't get en-twined.

The scimitar oryxes, who had much longer and sharper horns, watched in amazement. They wouldn't dare risk that sort of thing in case they stabbed each other. Most of the gazelles on board felt the same way.

There were many other antelopes with wonderful horns of all shapes and sizes, but these two, Hirolas, they were called, were the only ones to prance about neck to neck so much.

It was Archimedes, however, his handsome head of red hair bristling, whose pastime was by far the most intriguing. At first, it appeared he was just having fun. But, oh no, some serious mathematics had been going on, according to Archimedes himself, that was.

He would swing on a rope up to the crow's nest, which was simply an empty apple barrel attached to Pandora's old wooden mast, like the one the great Antarctic explorer Ernest Shackleton had on his boat, Quest, when he voyaged to the South Pole. After making some preparations, Archimedes would climb out, and, gripping the mast with just his hands, he would slide down to the deck, make some notes, then repeat the process. On one occasion, he slid down so fast, he landed with quite a thud on his bottom. Apparently, he had only been using one hand on that occasion, just to try the idea out. He stuck to two hands after that.

"Pandora's mast has been the perfect article for my experiment," Archimedes explained to Christopher, having finished his sliding activities, "and there can be no disputing my findings."

Christopher didn't have long to wait before his brother revealed those findings, although he couldn't say he was all that interested in knowing what they were.

"There can be no doubt," Archimedes bristled proudly like a true scientist, "that contrary to public belief, mango skin is quite a bit more slippery than banana skin. Paw paw skin comes third. Q.E.D."

Christopher stared at Archimedes vacantly. So that's what he had been doing.

Christopher was always suitably impressed by what his brother got up to, and by the way he expressed himself. But by and large, he would just shrug his shoulders and think, 'Whatever.' He had once been told what Q.E.D. stood for, but it had all sounded foreign to Christopher. He seemed to remember it meant something like: 'So there, proved it!'

Archimedes proceeded to explain the equations he had called upon to reach his stunning conclusions, but Christopher was soon lost. His only thought was of this 'pie' Archimedes kept referring to, being quite peckish. He let his brother have his moment though. "How clever you are, Colin - I mean, Archimedes. It's hard to believe we're twins. You're so clever and I'm so dim."

"It's merely a matter of study," Archimedes explained, thinking what he could work out next. "We're really quite the same except for that. I like studying and you don't. Q.E.D." he concluded, again leaving Christopher to ponder 'Q.E.D' again.

A good number of miracle berries were needed to keep the persistent calls of "Why?" from the young hyrax to a manageable level without her parents having to resort to too much invention. They found these "Why?'s" went away when she played with other small creatures, like the elephant shrews and bush-babies. The dik diks amused her as well, with their little horns and mohican hairstyles. They sometimes played jumping games to see who could go highest and longest. The dik diks usually won, with the bush babies a close second.

But everyone was sure to keep clear of the circuit runners every time they pounded by. The constant 'Hup, one, two, stretch! Hup, one two, stretch!' usually giving them fair warning.

The elephants were always on hand with a squirt from their trunks to cool anyone down who got too hot in the heat of the day whatever their exertions might have been. So they were soon everyone's friends.

Only Mr. Rhinoceros seemed not to be having a good time on holiday. He very often would just stand on his own looking back at Pandora's wake, as if missing home. The only thing that seemed to lift his gloom was when the blue whales showed themselves. He would watch them in wonderment. He knew he was quite a big animal himself, but these creatures were enormous. The biggest know mammals on earth.

One evening after all aboard had had their fill - or their fill of what the captain had allowed them, for it soon became apparent that the food was being strictly rationed - Mr. Rhinoceros got to his feet thoughtfully and officially introduced himself. His name was Rowland, with a 'W', not Roland, without a 'W'.

For most of the journey so far, he had kept himself to himself, resting most of the time in the shadow of Pandora's funnel. As the sun moved round, so did Mr. Rhinoceros, until it was almost directly above with little shade to be had. Then he would squeeze his rather bulky weight under which ever of the lifeboats had most room available out of the hot rays, which was usually the one with snoring coming from it. The mandrills chose that one, too. They found snoring was far more preferable to having dik diks and bush-babies jumping all over them while they groomed each other or being run down by Bono and his troupe.

Mr Rhinoceros spots a blue whale's tail

"Well, my friends,' Rowland began, breathing the cool evening air deeply in and exhaling with a satisfying flutter of his big wide lips. "Here we are on a beautiful steamship on a wonderful evening with the stars gleaming and the moon rising over a placid ocean, on our way to a new world for most of us I am sure. " He paused, took another deep breath, letting his lips flutter again as he let it out. "It is a world that we have heard so many inspiring things about, with so many sights to see. Well, let me tell you a little about myself." Here he paused again in deep thought, as if he was wondering whether he should say what he was about to say. There was a deadly hush on the deck. Even the snoring had stopped. The gathering was all ears.

CHAPTER 5

"I myself," Rowland went on, trying to compose himself, "have not really come on this cruise to relax and enjoy the sights of Europe. My main goal has been...errhum... how shall I put this without boring you all with things I'm sure you already know? Well, let me just say that we animals - not just in Africa, I might add - but it is Africa that concerns us, isn't it, being African? Apart from Mrs. Elephant, who is Asian by birth, but African by adoption, shall we say. By all accounts, I'm sure what I'm getting at applies as much to Asian animals as to African."

He paused again, with another fluttering deep breath, trying not to lose his train of thought. "Anyway, we animals have been having a hard time of it one way or another. One way being that over the years we have been pushed further and further off land that has always been ours to freely roam and settle on. Why? As Nosy the little hyrax might ask. To make way for the demands of Homo Sapiens, as in human beings. Let us call them Saps. People. Our forests are going, our habitat being destroyed. There are so many people now to feed, that our needs are being ignored. Equation: more people equals fewer animals. QED, as Archimedes might say."

This reference prompted a polite wave of recognition from the studious Colobus monkey. The 'another' way we animals have been suffering is more personal to me and, sadly, more woeful," Mr. Rhinoceros continued. "Indeed, it has been catastrophic. You see these horns on my head?" At this point he turned his head from side to side so that everyone could get a good look at his magnificent horns. "These horns are prized by some misguided Saps who believe that they have magical medicinal powers. But I can assure you that they do not. They are just like your hooves Mr. and Mrs. Zebra and your fingernails Mr. and Mrs. Bonobo. And these misguided individuals will kill to get their hands on these horns, my dear friends. They have been murdering us for centuries. So now, as I say, catastrophically, we are very few indeed."

There were sad nods all round, as other animals identified with what was being said.

"You notice," Rowland continued, "that there is only one of me on this cruise. I lost my darling, Rita, two years ago in the murderous manner I just mentioned. Two years! I shall never recover from that loss, but life must go on. It is time for me to rebuild; to try to pick up the pieces. I am no spring chicken, in fact I am quite old for a rhinoceros, having avoided the fate of others. I heard that these ocean cruises often opened up opportunities of meeting new partners, even for those getting on in years. But sadly, this is not going to happen on this trip. I shall have to rely on your friendly companionship to help me enjoy the sights of...."

Rowland was struggling to finish the sentence, for he had become too emotional to get the words out. Seeing this, Vernon, the vervet monkey, stepped up and gently wiped away his tears.

"Rowland has said it all," Mr. Elephant took the moment to speak. "He has summed up our domestic situation to a T." Some of the animals wondered what the 'T' meant, but nevertheless understood the point being made.

"Yes, indeed," Hyacinth, Nosy's mother agreed. "He has put it in a nutshell." she added at once, realizing she had chosen her words badly, because she got an immediate response from Nosy, which was quickly dealt with.

"That is such a sad story, Rowland," Grevy, Mr. Zebra said, comforting his son, Zach, who like some of the others was close to tears. "We won't be feeling quite so sorry for ourselves now, will we, Zoe?"

Mrs. Zebra agreed. "At least we have each other and our lovely Zach."

"But it has to be said that we've had to face up to vanishing numbers ourselves," Grevy went on. "Perhaps if we didn't have such stripy skins, we wouldn't end up as carpets and rugs so often."

As Grevy uttered these disturbing remarks, Zoe covered little Zach's ears, shushing Mr. Zebra with a stern look. Zach was upset enough already by Rowland's story without hearing of their own woes. Zoe could always tell when Zach was upset, because his magnificent mane, which normally stood bushily straight up, would flop to one side. And it was flopping now. "Yes, well, as Zoe has said" Grevy hesitated, suitably told off, "we consider ourselves very lucky to have each other, at least."Zoe gave him a tight-lipped glance. Enough said.

"Like Mr. and Mrs. Zebra," Hildegard, the very pretty hirola antelope who liked dancing volunteered, "Hugh and I think ourselves very fortunate, too, considering everything."

It seemed as if Hildegard was wearing white spectacles. But in fact it was just white fur around the eyes that looked like very attractive designer glasses.

"Yes, Hildegard, my dear," Hugh agreed readily, looking very studious, because he was actually wearing proper spectacles with black frames covering the white fur. The lenses were slightly rose-tinted, like sunglasses. He was obviously well prepared for his holiday. "We hirolas, Hildegard and I, as I expect you all know, are antelopes, like all the impalas, gazelles and dik diks here, not deer, which, when used as a plural word, funnily doesn't have an 's' at the end. And you can tell the difference by our horns, which are more or less straight in us antelopes. Deer have antlers which are like the branches of a tree." Hugh ducked his head and moved it side to side as Mr.

Rhinoceros had done to show off his horns, which, although fairly straight, had an attractive wiggly shape to them. Then he proceeded to make an unexpected announcement.

"Just so all of you know, Hildegard and I are on our honeymoon!"

Cries of congratulations stopped him for a moment, but then he went on dreamily: "This cruise seemed too good to refuse. What a good opportunity to relax and contemplate our life together. We have big decisions to make. We might have to relocate when we get back from this trip, for example. What's been said here goes for us hirolas as well. There are so few of us left."

"Too true," Hildegard agreed. "Hugh and I both roamed and roamed before we were lucky enough to find each other. I had almost given up. And then, there he was, standing in the shade of a lone tree that seemed to have escaped those heavy machines that churn up the land."

"She came running over to me, the breeze in her mane, and it was love at first sight. She was so pretty."

"And he was so handsome, with his big powerful horns almost reaching the branches above."

They looked fondly at each other, and then Hugh, realizing they were perhaps being a bit too lovy-dovy in the circumstances, turned back to the gathering and went on: "And it is hard to accept that these great horns of ours are to be blamed in no small way for our own troubles. But unlike Rowland's horns that are ground up to make fake medicine, ours are sought as 'trophies'! Just to be hung on the wall and shown off."

"The ways of some Saps must often be a mystery to themselves." Mr. Elephant's rich deep voice offered, lifting his trunk high in the air to expose his gloriously long and pointed tusks to their best advantage. "With us elephants, it has been these tusks, this ivory, that they hunt us for. And we all know to what lengths they will go to get their hands on them." Here he paused and turned to Ella, his baby daughter, before continuing. "It has also been known, if you can believe it, that our left ears are often cut off as trophies! If you notice, my left ear is the shape of Africa." Again, there was a moment of demonstration. When everyone had had a good look at his 'African' ear, he went on: "This is the reason we are so pleased that Ella has an Asian left ear; neither the shape of Africa nor India."

He waited until everyone had compared all the differently shaped ears before adding: "But on a happier note, there are many good people out there trying to help us. So, let us be happy that not all homo sapiens are bad. And let this be said: a growing number lot of those who care about animals are children! This really is good news for our survival. Our best hope."

CHAPTER 6

"That is something that might bring hope for the future, as you say," a voice like the sound of a piccolo trumpet intervened, "But right now the news is not so bright for us wee hippos." It came from one of the baby hippopotamuses that had come aboard without a grown-up. Mrs. Elephant had been quite concerned about this, as it happened, since she was very protective of her baby, Ella.

"My name is Pip, and this is Petra, my other half," the hippo went on, encouraging Petra to get to her feet and do a little curtsy. And it was a little curtsy, for like Pip, the other other half, she had very short legs. "Well, Petra and I have been together for several years, and we haven't stopped moving from place to place since we met. Why? I'll ask that myself, Nosy. The answer is to keep ahead of the loggers and hunters that are a danger to all of us." He did a cumbersome twirl around Petra. "You see how plump and cuddly we are?" he said, coming to a stop facing the wrong way, but quickly correcting himself with a gentle bump of his fat tummy against Petra's equally fat backside. "Well, we must be very tasty, because 'you know who' very much likes to eat us. That is why it is such a relief to be on this cruise in one safe place without having to keep running. And it's for more than one reason..."

31

He was just about to add something, when the words 'bush meat' were uttered. They came from a chimpanzee, or was it a bonobo, they were so similar, and they quickly echoed around the various groups of monkeys and apes gathered. Monkeys and apes knew all about being hunted for what was called 'bush meat'.

Listening to what the little hippopotamus, had been saying, Mr. Elephant interrupted with a certain hesitation, hoping not to hurt Pip and Petra's feelings, and said: "If I might be cheeky and ask you something that has been puzzling Mrs. Elephant and I. You say you've been together for years, but to us you seemed to be orphaned baby hippos."

Pip and Petra looked at each other and burst out laughing, which brought some welcome relief to everyone after hearing so many distressing stories. It was such a comic, engaging laughter. It sounded like a school brass band tuning up, mixed with the last drips of water draining from a bath.

"We are definitely not babies," Pip announced with a gaping grin which revealed how large his mouth was. "We are grown-ups. But we are not your regular hippopotamuses, we are SPECIAL!" He took a moment to allow this last declaration to sink in. "We are none other than PYGMY hippopotamuses! Both fully grown, I can assure you. But if you want to see a baby hippo, you might not have to wait too long. I was about to tell you, but," he turned to Petra. "You tell them, Petra."

Petra blushed, and said, "No, you tell them." Secretly, Petra was very shy and embarrassed by the sound of her own gurgly voice. She was quite happy to let Pip do all the talking.

By now, most of the animals had guessed what was coming. They were ready to clap and cheer as soon as Pip announced that Petra was pregnant. "We're so happy about it. And happier still now to be in one place for a while so Petra doesn't have the anxiety of rushing about avoiding hunters."

"Well, that's some good news, at least," said Gerald, Mr. Giraffe. "Let's be thankful for that." He had been thinking of telling his tale of woe along with his distant cousins, the Okapi's. But that could wait for another day.

"Us pangolins also have some good news," Pascal let it be known, sliding his son off his back. "But not much. I'll come to that in a minute. First the bad news. You wouldn't think to look at us with these hard shiny scales that anyone would want to eat us. We don't look as tasty as our cuddly little hippo friends here. But, if you can imagine it, we are considered to be very tasty; a delicacy indeed! And there is more bad news, because these hard, shiny scales of ours are prized by some members of the Sap species for having similar magical properties as Mr. Rhino's spectacular horns. Again, not so. They are just like finger nails, only much bigger. And I suppose they do have a magical quality of sorts, which brings us back to the good news. Let me demonstrate.

He motioned to Philomena, Mrs. Pangolin, whose daughter was on her back - obviously the little ones' favourite place to sit - and bid them form a line. With the young ones in the middle, the four of them moved centre stage, so to speak, so that everyone had a good view of what was about to happen. "You know the routine, children," Pascal said confidently, with a nod to Philomena.

And without further ado, Pascal yelled: "Alarm!!!"

Suddenly, all that was left were four shiny balls, two big ones and two smaller ones, rocking back and forth to Pandora's gentle swell.

"Amazing!" everyone cried. "Fantastic." "Where have they gone?" "Well, I never!" "What magic!" "Why?"

There was no end to the wonderment, until suddenly Pascal unwound himself and was back again on all fours. "Philomena," he cried, and there she was again. "Children!" And up they popped, just like synchronized swimmers.

"That my friends," Pascal announced proudly. "Is the good news of how we protect ourselves in what I would call our normal world. But, of course, that technique is of no use when we don't see danger coming, as in a poacher's trap or a hunter's bullet. So, I say to all the Saps out there, 'If you think horns and scales can cure your ills, chew on your fingernails. You'll get the same negative result.'"

Then he announced proudly, "I wrote a song about this," and proceeded to sing it before anyone could choose otherwise, tap-dancing at the same time.

> We pangolins are pretty neat
>
> With shiny scales and nifty feet
>
> If danger comes we fool you all
>
> By disappearing into balls
>
> Hear this, we have a tale to tell
>
> That's A-L-E not A-I-L
>
> To all you Saps who prize our scales
>
> They're made of stuff just like your nails
>
> Now here's the crunch so wise up Saps
>
> Stop your poaching then perhaps
>
> You'll help to stop a tragic end
>
> And show there is no magic blend
>
> Of ground down tusks or horns or scales
>
> You might as well just chew your

nails

Although the words conveyed a serious message, the melody in Pascal's song was quite jolly, the rattling of his scales as he tap-danced keeping time just like a snare drum. To finish, he jumped into the air, turned into a ball momentarily, then unwound himself as he came down to land on his feet and take a bow.

It took a while for the clapping to stop. When it did, Mr. Rhinoceros, still nodding in appreciation of Pascal's insightful song, considered his thoughts for a moment and concluded: "It's not that all Saps are bad and misguided. We know they are not. There are groups out there who really care. And we have hope that the concern of their children stays with them till old age. But for now, without going over it all again, our situation is not good."

Wanting to end the night on a happier note, Arthur, the Aardvark said jauntily: "Well at least we have found one of the good Saps in our captain. How generous of him to arrange this all-inclusive holiday cruise for us absolutely free of charge."

"Excuse me?" a strange voice snapped loudly from somewhere. "Did I hear someone say 'Free of charge'? You gotta be kidding me?"

Chuck peeps out at his travelling companions

CHAPTER 7

The voice was coming from one of the lifeboats; the snoring one. From a furry head that was peeping over the side of it.

So that was who had been sleeping there all the time!

"I'm Chuck," the furry creature introduced himself. "As you can probably guess from my lingo, I'm not from Africa. I'm from the US of A! And I'm kinda embarrassed, 'cos I slipped aboard when I saw all you guys following that Sap, as I heard you calling 'em, you know, the one carrying the flag with 'Sight-Seeing Cruise to Europe' on it. What can I say? I've been on my travels. And right then I had to make a quick decision on how to go about continuing my adventures. When I saw you all lined up destination Europe, easy choice. But let me tell ya, I kinda thought I was sneaking aboard Pandora as a stowaway, you know, without having to pay. But now you tell me it's gratis! As in zilch! Which I find hard to believe. Us yanks, er, that's Americans, have always been told that there ain't no such thing as a free lunch, so to speak. Free cruise? No way, hozay! Something's up. Big time! And, sorry, couldn't do much about it, I've been ear-wigging all your stories. Wow! That's bad vibes, man! You guys are sure in some sort of fix." "But if you're from, er, the US of A," Mr. Elephant inquired, "how come you ended up in Africa?"

"Well, there's another story for ya, buddy," Chuck replied with a clicking sound from his lips. "I was just about to wise you up." Feeling more confident now, he edged himself up and sat on the side of the lifeboat, holding onto one of the rowlocks. "I can hardly believe it myself, ya know."

Now that he had exposed himself fully, it was easy to see he could be mistaken for a hyrax. A big one, though.

"Okay," Chuck continued, holding his paws out as if to own up." I'll shoot straight from the hip. I came from the US as a stowaway, just as I guess I am right now, or as I thought I was. But suddenly it's all got different, ya know, 'gratis' and all that don't exactly tie in with being a stowaway. I ain't too comfortable with this 'zilch' theory just yet, though. Ya kidding me!? You get nothin' for nothin' where I come from!'"

The animals were unfamiliar with some of Chuck's words, but they liked his openness and he had gained their interest.

"Anyway, let me tell ya, dudes, it was pure stowaway stuff coming from the States, and definitely 'gratis'." Chuck now had their full attention. "Let me explain. In case you hadn't guessed it, I'm a groundhog - or a woodchuck, or whistling pig, take your pick. We get called lots of other things as well. We guys usually hibernate during the winter months -

and let me tell ya, my body clock is all over the place at the moment. That's why I've been napping under the planks of this lifeboat since I came aboard. I couldn't tell you what day or hour it is, right now. Anyway, and you ain't gonna believe this. Listen up. Some rock and roll band - I guess you've heard of rock and roll music, that's gotta be everywhere these days. Well this band was doing a big open air concert and rigged their stage right over the burrow in the park where I live. And let me tell ya, they were so loud, they must have woken every hibernating groundhog from the Bronx to Vegas. They had a catchy name, this band. Sort of turned 'Rock and Roll' round to make it 'The Rolling Rocks'. Anyway, they were on this world tour, and their next stop was Africa. Well, I've always had the wander lust, so, I thought, Africa? Why not? The rest was easy. I just holed up in one of the bands RR packing cases and snoozed my way across the Atlantic. And here I am, even if my body clock ain't."

"That is some story. And you seem to have been snoozing quite a bit since you've been with us, I might add." chuckled Harry the hyrax, who could see a similarity in Chuck's looks to his own, but for the two small tusk-like teeth.

"Snoring?" Chuck suggested, getting smiling nods all round. "Yeah. I've been told."

"Well, you don't have to hide up there anymore," Harry said. "This trip is 'gratis' whether you're a stowaway or not. We're all in the same boat, to coin a phrase!"

"Well, thank you, thank you," Chuck said gratefully, the smiles and nods all round making him feel at home. "But I'll stay up here for the night, if that's OK. I think I can squeeze in a bit more shut-eye. And I ain't too sure of that captain guy just yet. Don't know what he'd make of a yankee groundhog in his midst." He shook his head thoughtfully. "Free holiday? Nope. I ain't buying it. Something's up, I tell ya."

As everyone curled up for the night, Chuck lay back and looked up at the stars. Before long he closed his eyes on them.

And then he was snoring again.

CHAPTER 8

When the animals gathered for breakfast the next morning, they were in for a shock.

"The food store is locked," Pascal reported. It was his job along with the vervet monkeys to take care of breakfast preparations. "The captain hasn't come out of his cabin yet."

"That's a bit off!" Bunny and Monty complained in unison. They were brother and sister Riverine rabbits, in that order, who looked as though they were smiling like Cheshire cats all the time. But they weren't. A line of black fur across their cheeks gave that impression. They had extremely long ears which flapped like wings and whiskers like propellers that always seemed to be twitching madly, as if they were about to take off. "We're quite peckish this morning."

"We're hungry, too," came a chorus from equally hungry mouths. "We didn't get allowed much to eat last night."

"Who needs food, when you have love?" Hugh mused, looking dreamily at Hildegard through his rose-tinted glasses.

"You'll soon find out if you have any little 'uns!" Mercedes ventured without turning her head. She was standing erect in the bow, keeping watch on the ocean. "Merlin! Check the children are in order," she beckoned by habit as Bono trundled past with his troupe. Merlin jumped to it, but unnecessarily as it happened. The children, and there were quite a few of them, were already formed in a perfect 'V' shape to either side of their mother mimicking her watchfulness.

"Has anyone knocked on the Sap's cabin door to tell him what's what?" Chuck asked, chuckling at Mercedes' bossiness.

"He doesn't like anyone doing that," said Wally, a warthog who couldn't seem to get all his teeth into his mouth. "Spoils his concentration, he told me the one time I did it. I thought he was going to throttle me!"

"What's he doing down there all the time?" Chuck pried. "Anyone know?"

"Sounds like he's doing a lot of tap dancing to me," a bushbaby called Busby, thought. "And I don't have to put my ear to the door to hear it, either."

"I think I know exactly what that is, Busby," Chuck said. "He's tapping on a computer key-pad. Now why would he be doing that all the time?"

"Perhaps he's writing a log" Petra, the pregnant pygmy hippo gurgled, immediately wishing she hadn't. Her words nevertheless puzzled a cluster of young monkeys. How on earth could you write with a log, they were wondering. That was something big to play on.

"Ya kidding me!?" Chuck questioned. "All day long? No, it ain't no log, I betcha. Has anyone managed to get a sly look into his cabin?"

There were shaking heads all round. "He double locks it, whether he's in it or not," Busby knew for sure. "Exactly," agreed Arthur. "He doesn't like anyone going near it, which I'm actually quite pleased about. I wouldn't want to be in there with him, or even without him. He came out once while I was in the corridor, and I wouldn't want to describe the smell that followed him, and the smoke. More saps like him in the rain forest, and we'd smell 'em a mile off."

"Two miles, more like," Wally ventured. "And it's not just the tobacco he smokes."

Chuck gave it some thought before speaking. "OK, let's try something. And if it works, the idea might be a handy trick to have up our sleeve."

The hungry animals looked at Chuck, intrigued to learn what he was planning.

"What can I tell ya? You guys might be smelling smoke and whatever, but I smell a rat. And that's saying something, coming from another rodent, as in yours truly. It takes one to know one!" he expressed gaily.

He set about explaining how they might get the captain to come out of his cabin so they could confront him about breakfast. At the same time, they could maybe get a peek inside if he forgot to lock it.

The secret was the satellite dish.

"The Sap mentioned it had to be pointing in the right direction to get a signal for his computer," he reminded them. "What we gotta do is change its angle somehow, so the screen goes blank."

"The dish is fixed ever so tightly," Bono revealed, rubbing one of his biceps. "I bumped into it doing circuits last night and it didn't budge. We'd need a big spanner to shift it."

"Which we don't have, right?"

They didn't.

There was only one way to do it. Steer Pandora off course.

But they would have to get her back on the compass line by the time the captain came on deck. "Know what I mean? Don't want the Sap suspecting what we're up to."

Busby would be in the corridor listening in on the captain tapping at the computer keys. A line of communication would be set up that went straight to Christopher who would be at the steering wheel.

Archimedes had worked out, quote, 'the most strategic locations for the chain of command to be stationed for the most effective and speediest passage of information' unquote. More simply, where the animals should position themselves.

"Archie, buddy," Chuck addressed Archimedes, "help us out, here. We need timings?"

They needed to know roughly how long it would take the captain to come out of his cabin, lock the door, or, better still, not lock the door, then negotiate the corridors and stairs before reaching the steering wheel position.

Archimedes rose to the task, making his way immediately with deliberate steps to the stairs that lead to below deck. Several minutes later he reappeared. After making some calculations, he announced, "Based on assessments of the captain's speed of waddle and the number of 180 degree corridor turns, plus the number and accumulation of stairs with the rise and slope of each step duly measured and noted, I would estimate this time to be in the region of 97 seconds."

Archimedes took even greater pains to explain how he had worked out that it would take less than a second for the command signal to go from one end of the line to the other. This being because the wave of the hand would travel at the speed of light to the person watching, and so on down the line – or in this case, up the line. Therefore, as long as everyone was paying attention and waved instantaneously Christopher would get his cue at the steering wheel, give or take a millionth of a second, for the time it took light to travel 203 feet, the distance Archimedes had just paced out from where Busby would be standing. "So, if..."

Before Archimedes could go on to divide 203 feet by 186,000 miles (the speed of light per second) which was a lot of feet, Chuck stopped him.

"OK, OK, give us a break, Archie. So, what ya saying is, it'll be pretty quick. So we'll have about 97 seconds to get Pandora back on course." He gave it some thought, then added: "Sounds a bit tight, but, Bono, if you and your troupe just happened to be taking a time-out at the top of the stairs in the captain's way, that could delay him a few more seconds. What do you say?"

Bono was only too happy to oblige. With all this talk about evil Saps, he was extra keen to show whose side he was on since he was so close to being a homo sapien himself. "Consider it done!" he confirmed with a salute, turning smartly to round up his team.

The number of animals needed were placed strategically where they could see each other to pass on the signal and waited for Busby to conceal himself. Being so small, he hid himself in a fire bucket hanging close to the captain's cabin.

The tap tapping was already echoing along the corridor, so Busby waved straight away to Vernon, next in line, who quickly passed the signal along.

As Archimedes had anticipated, Christopher received his cue almost immediately and steered Pandora 10 degrees off course.

Everyone waited with baited breath, but no second signal came to say the captain had left his cabin. He was still on the computer.

"20 degrees!" Chuck ordered after a minute had passed. Christopher steered 20 degrees off course.

Below decks, the tap, tap tapping suddenly stopped, to be replaced by loud curses. Busby, shaking with anticipation, pressed himself down into the sand of the fire bucket and listened. He heard the lock being turned and the captain coming out. Would he or wouldn't he lock the door as he left? Busby held his breath. The answer was 'yes', he would lock it. With great relief, Busby waved down the line to Vernon and stopped shaking. If the captain hadn't locked the door, it was his job to sneak into the cabin for a quick look round. Something he hadn't at all fancied doing, not just because of the smell. The waves passed along the line quickly until they reached Hugh - who was in the last position before Christopher at the wheel - and hit a problem.

Hildegard had come to join Hugh and they had started necking! This made Hugh miss his signal from Harry, who was soon waving and hissing frantically. In the end it took a muffled cry to alert Hugh about what he was supposed to be doing before Christopher finally got the signal and pulled Pandora back on course, whistling as if nothing untoward had happened.

Even with Hugh's incompetence, there had been no real urgency. The captain had struggled so much with all the stairs that he didn't appear on deck till more than a minute later than Archimedes had expected. "Well, he's obviously not as fit as I thought he was," was how Archimedes excused his miscal-culation "He smokes too much and should lose some weight. A few circuits with Bono would not go amiss," he added sarcastically, as Bono led his troupe off with a 'Hup, one, two, stretch!' after their false time-out.

Once on deck, the captain had gone first to the sat-ellite dish, to see that it hadn't come loose. It wasn't until minutes later that he went to check Pandora was on the correct compass line. And since she was, he had nothing to complain about.

But the animals did. They surrounded him on deck and were asking him about breakfast.

"Ah, yes," the captain bluffed. "With all these goings on, it slipped my mind." "Pull the other one, knucklehead," Chuck muttered under his breath, listening from the confines of his lifeboat. He was definitely happier staying invisible to the captain.

"I'll go down and open the store," the captain prom-ised. "But first I must see about something in my cabin." He then added with a forced smile, "Why don't you all make yourselves busy today. Give this old boat a wash and brush up. And has no-one come up with any exciting acts yet? It would be in their best interest." More than you would ever know, he was thinking to himself slyly. "I've told you, more food for anyone with the right talent to entertain me! How good would that be?"

With that, he descended the stairs to his cabin.

CHAPTER 9

After breakfast, some of the tidier animals did as the captain had suggested and set about giving Pandora a clean-up.

Mrs. Giraffe asked Mrs. Okabi if she fancied helping her with sweeping the decks. The okabis were quite close relations to giraffes, although their necks weren't nearly so long. From behind, okabis actually looked quite like zebras, with their bottoms covered with stunning black and white stripes.

They started by brushing the dust from the nooks and crannies on the decks, clearing the way for Mrs. Elephant to wash them down with squirts from her trunk. The younger animals loved this, getting in the way of the spray to cool themselves down or to be pushed across the deck as if on a slide.

Mercedes got Merlin to oversee all this. "Make sure none of those kids get washed overboard," she ordered

It didn't take long before Pandora's decks had been tidied up and things returned to normal, although Bono and his troupe hadn't stopped their normal activity of doing circuits while all the cleaning had been going on.

Hugh and Hildegard hadn't stopped their normal activity either. Cuddling each other with their necks entwined, occasionally sighing and looking out to sea. They were in their own blissful world.

Mercedes went to join Chuck who was chatting to some of the others about how little food they were getting and how much of it was left in storage below decks. The feeling was supplies wouldn't last unless they stopped somewhere to restock within the next few days.

"So how long have we been going, 4 or 5 days?" Chuck wanted to know. "I'm only guessing from what you guys have been saying. I've no idea how long I was asleep before your stories woke me up."

"6 days," Mr. Elephant enlightened Chuck.

"And food's running short already?"

"No doubt about it."

At the mention of food, others joined the group.

Chuck took his time to respond. "As I see it," he speculated, "we gotta take a look in that cabin real fast. See what's going on. So, OK, we know how to get the Sap out, but how do we get in? That's our problem. We can't solve this thing until we know exactly what the schmuck's up to. But what I can tell ya is that one way or another you've been conned. And I think that's putting it mildly."

Those around him were nodding. They knew what he was saying.

"It seems to me, listening to you all shooting the breeze the other night," Chuck went on, "that you guys are precious. You gotta look out for each other. It sounds like things ain't too rosy for you back home, with all your tales of woe - some so woe-ish... hey! What can I say? It's a wonder some of you are still around! I can see, ya know, how you took this knucklehead of a Sap at his word. I mean, just to get away from all your troubles for a bit. Take Mr. Rhinoceros's story, for instance, and forgive my ignorance, is he a black or a white rhino, would anyone know? He's so calm and peaceful for such a big dude, in spite of his problems."

"He is definitely a white one," Gerald, the giraffe, answered straight out. "Even though he's the first one I've ever seen and he's not really white; more like grey. I've come across a few black ones in my time, although, again, they're closer to being grey. Unlike Mr. White Rhino, the black ones have got really funny looking droopy lips, although I wouldn't say that directly to their face. I met one once when he was angry, and you couldn't see me for dust. Mr. White Rhino is like a lamb in comparison."

"You got it, buddy. Soft as velvet," Chuck agreed, pursing his lips and clicking while his line of thought came back to him. "Yeah, well, my woes ain't worth dog-poo compared to what I heard from you guys the other night. Apologies, for my language. What can I say? Put it this way, there ain't no shortage of us rodents. We're all over the place. And not just rats, mice, and guinea pigs. Take the capybara. Now there's a rodent for ya! What a size! And there's one little dude, an agouti, he's called, who they reckon is the main reason so many nut trees grow in Brazil. It seems our little agouti rodent ain't got much of a memory, so when he buries a nut he forgets where he's put it, so it stays buried and grows. No Brazilian Sap is going to eat an agouti, unless he's a real stupid Sap. Oh, yeah, the stupid ones are out there, for sure. But, I can promise you, us rodents don't grace the table of many Saps. We ain't that tasty, for starters," he chuckled. "Or for a main course come to that! And whoever heard of a coat or carpet being made out of rat fur? Come on! Ya kidding me?"

Chuck's frankness and way of talking brought more smiles all round. Attention turned back to the problem of getting into the captain's cabin. It seemed that it didn't take equations to figure it out.

Chuck looked at Archimedes, then at Christopher, then at Mercedes, and finally at Harry.

"Are we all thinking the same thing?" he asked, getting nods all round. "The only way in is through the..."

"Port hole!" they all whispered, bunching up to give a high five, which was more like a low five for Harry. Despite being a distant cousin of the elephant family, he couldn't reach quite as far up as the other four

"So, who gets the job?" Chuck put to the conclave.

Bunny and Monty with their big ears had clearly heard what had been passing between the five. Immediately, they went into their guitar string trembling mode, except only an anxious whimper came out. 'Please don't let it be one of us!' it was saying.

"Someone small enough to get through the port hole." Chuck stated.

"Someone with big eyes in case there's no light in the cabin." Followed Christopher.

"Someone with good hearing, in case danger approaches." Was Harry's offering.

"Someone with a good grip, to avoid falling into the sea." Mercedes suggested wisely.

"Someone who can jump well enough to get onto desks and cupboards." Archimedes considered.

"And someone whose smell ain't too great, or whose nose can take a peg!" Chuck concluded, accompanied by gales of laughter as all five of them turned to Busby.

"Who, me?" Busby gaped, looking from one to the other of the nodding five conspirators.

"Gotta be, buddy," Chuck stressed before Busby could make a case for himself. "You've got all the talents needed, not forgetting how intelligent you are."

"But I can smell things perfectly!" Busby protested.

"You'll be needing a peg, then," the gang decided.

It was no use objecting further. The conspiracy was underway and Busby was already being hailed as a hero for volunteering to do the entering.

CHAPTER 10

There was just the little matter of keeping the captain out of his cabin for long to give Busby enough time to make the scheme successful.

"And I think I know how it can be done." Chuck announced, drawing everyone's attention. "I've been juggling with the idea since the schmuck mentioned he'd like to see some tricks. Got my drift?"

"Gotcha!" Archimedes twigged, courtesy of a Chuckism. "While the cat's on deck watching the tricks, the mouse will play. Or in this case, the bushbaby."

"Q.E.D.!" Chuck responded, cheekily, to get his own back. "So? Who can juggle, for a start?"

A discussion went round the gathering as to who seemed most likely to have that skill and the vervet monkeys came top of the list. Vernon said he would put a team together and have a go at arranging something. But no promises. First they would have to find something to juggle with.

Vernon's youngest son, suggested bananas. But it was thought the captain wouldn't go for that idea in case some went missing.

"We'll try to come up with something," Vernon reassured the group, taking his family aside to consider possibilities. "Pascal and Philomena could do their disappearance act!" Busby blurted out, getting into the swing of things now he was being looked upon as a hero. "That's a terrific trick. The captain will probably want to see that over and over again."

"There ya go, Busby, buddy," Chuck congratulated him. "More suggestions like that and you'll have plenty of time to nose around the cabin, even with a peg on it!"

While heads were being put together to come up with tricks that might grab the captain's attention, the high five five, more correctly, the high five four and a half, set about the major mission of getting Busby into the cabin and safely out of it again. There were several port holes along the side of Pandora and they had to make sure Busby went into the right one. Archimedes had immediately started pacing out distances again, but his friends saved him the effort. One look over the side revealed exactly which port hole they were looking for; the only one with smoke coming out of it!

"We're gonna have to lower Busby over the side with a rope," Chuck stated the obvious. "Tie a loop and tuck it under his arms so there's no danger of it slipping off."

"Quite! We don't want to lose you into the deep, Busby," Archimedes said. Then added unhelpfully, "And I would estimate that it is very deep indeed."

"Even if it was only a foot deep, we wouldn't want to lose our Busby, would we? He ain't that big," Chuck pointed out, noticing Busby gulping at the thought of what he had let himself in for. 'Did I really volunteer for this?' he was asking himself.

"We should tie the rope securely to the deck at the top end," Mercedes suggested. "With the exact length to reach down to the port hole. Just in case it slips out of our hands as we lower him."

Another gulp from Busby. More audible this time.

"I'll calculate what length of rope we need," Archimedes offered gladly. Then added rather inappropriately: "Any particular colour, Busby?"

"Just make it strong," were the only words Busby could think of to answer such a silly question.

"You're gonna have to slip out of the loop once you get inside the cabin, Buzz, buddy," Chuck was thinking. "It'll hamper your movements and might knock things over, and we can't have that. Just have a good nose around. If the Sap senses one of us has been in there, the game'll be up. We'll have the line of command in position if he for some reason decides to return to the cabin while you're still in it. So if you hear a knock on the door, scarper quick."

"Make sure when you slip out of the loop to hang it over the port hole cover, so it doesn't blow out of your reach when you need it to come up again," Christopher said astutely. "One of us will be ready at the other end. Just give the rope a couple of little tugs when you've got the loop under your arms, and we'll pull you up. What do you weigh? No more than a pound of bananas, I bet?"

To give Christopher a better idea, Busby jumped unexpectedly up into his hands. This leap impressed the mission conspirators greatly. It was many times higher than Busby himself!

Christopher pretended to weigh him by bouncing him gently in his palms. "Okay," he assessed. "Not much more than one banana!"

"Wow!" Chuck chuckled. "What a jump! Are you the right guy for this job or what? You betcha!" The diminutive figure peering out from between Christopher's fingers was gloating proudly at the success of his jump. "And what a tail!"

Hanging down from Christopher's hands, Busby's tail was much longer than his body.

"Betta watch out for that as well when you're in the cabin, Buzzy boy," Chuck warned. "Don't want no mishaps there."

To prove he had complete control of his long tail, Busby made it stand up in a spiral, then turned it into a square, then tickled Christopher's ears with it using it like a paint brush before making it disappear underneath his body. "How's that?" He wanted to know, and that was just dandy, according to Chuck.

CHAPTER 11

Before the campaign could start, they had to be certain enough tricks were at the ready to keep the captain on deck long enough for Busby to have a good look around the cabin.

"What have we got?" Chuck asked around hopefully.

The vervet monkeys couldn't find anything to juggle with, but had come up with a swinging act using some of Pandora's rigging. It wouldn't be very exciting, but it was a start. It was either that or a kind of monkey pyramid.

"Bono, buddy. What can you give us?"

"Maybe I can get the team skipping, something like that." Bono offered. "What about a tug-o-war?"

"Hey! There ya go. Could be good. A bit of 'hup, one, two, tug' might go down well."

Hugh and Hildegard, the honeymooners, weren't too sure why they were being asked to think of something to do. They hadn't really been paying attention to the doubts that had been growing amongst some of the other animals, and perhaps that was a good thing. But they loved to dance and said it would be their pleasure to perform an Argentinian tango for the captain. "He is taking us on holiday, after all."

"Whatever," Chuck responded quietly not wanting to disillusion them. He sent Christopher a knowing glance that spoke volumes. "A tango sounds promising."

But what would seal it, the conspirators were thinking, was Pascal's troupe of disappearing pangolins. That and an inspirational game of ten pin bowling that Mercedes had come up with.

By the early afternoon they were ready.

"Let's do it" Chuck gave the word. With a final high five, they set about getting the captain out of his cabin. Everyone went to his position in the line of command and Christopher took Pandora immediately to 20 degrees off course. In less than 2 minutes the captain was at the satellite dish and Pandora was back on course.

"I don't know what's going on with this signal!" the captain muttered after a brief look at the compass to check their direction. "The satellite itself must be having a wobbly, I suppose. There's nothing wrong with the weather."

They had chosen Diana, the sweetest little dik dik, to approach him before he went down the stairs. "Mr. Captain, sir," she said to him as prompted. "We have lots of lovely tricks for you to see, as you requested. We've got them all ready for you. We have a chair in the best position back there where there is enough space." She motioned to an area they had chosen for the tricks away from the trick being prepared behind his back above the port hole.

"Yes, yes. Very good," he said.

By now, Busby had come up from his position in the line of command outside the captain's cabin and was slipping into the looped rope.

With the captain sitting in the selected place, Archimedes took great pains in making a long introduction to the forthcoming acts to allow more time for the all important rope trick about to happen on the other side of the boat.

"Get on with it." the captain ordered, bored with Archimedes long words. "What's first?"

The vervet monkeys presented themselves, seven of them, and to start with they did some rope swinging; fairly ordinary rope swinging compared to what they normally did in the rain forest. So that didn't go down too well. There main act was to construct a small pyramid; three of them at the bottom, two standing on their shoulders, one on theirs with the smallest of them standing atop holding her hands high as if cheering.

"Hmm," the captain muttered. "Next!"

On the other side of Pandora, Busby had reached the target port hole. He had decided against the peg, and was wondering if that had been wise. For all the talk of a smell was still true. And it wasn't just smoke. There was also a sort of metallic pong mixed in with human ones.

He took a deep breath before slipping inside, not forgetting to hook the loop of the rope over the port hole cover. Before delving further, he took a quick look around the cabin from where he was. And froze!

The vervet monkeys hadn't impressed the captain at all. 'I need something much better than that!' he was thinking.

Next up were the hirolas, Hugh and Hildegard. Because they had no music to dance to, they asked the animals to beat out a tango rhythm. Although they were clearly enjoying themselves prancing around on the deck, with wild swings and necking, the captain put a quick stop to it.

Bono's skipping troupe didn't impress him either, mainly because the only pieces of rope they could find for the job were too thick and heavy for some of the smaller hands.

The tug-of-war contest didn't live up to promise, either. When Bono shouted: "Hup, one, two, tug!" nothing moved. The teams were so evenly matched, it was more like a tug-of-peace.

"Tricks, I want. Tricks! Think circus!" the captain roared ill-temperedly. It was obvious he was losing patience. His face was beginning to screw up and his wild beard started swinging from side to side as if caught in a storm.

In the cabin, Busby had recovered from the shock of what he had first seen. He was now able to take a closer look. In front of him on a desk was a humming computer screen. It was blank, apart from some funny looking blinking things at the top of it. On the wall behind it hung a framed photograph. It was this photograph and what was lying on the desk under it that had taken Busby's breath away.

Busby shudders when he sees the picture on the cabin wall

Guns! Big, long guns. Two of them, with what looked like telescopes fixed to them. There were boxes of ammunition piled alongside them, some of them with pictures that looked like darts on them. The photograph was of the grinning captain, gun in hand, with his foot resting on the tusk of an elephant lying lifeless on the ground in a pool of blood!

Back on deck, Mercedes was anxious to keep the captain's attention going, because there had been no sign that Busby was ready to come up. "I think you'll find this next trick to your liking, Mr. Captain. You can have a go at it yourself, should you wish. It's a sort of hands on type of trick." Mercedes had to take a deep breath to address the captain with such false politeness. But she had managed it effectively.

With Merlin in pole position, Mercedes selected nine of her children to stand stiffly behind him like pins in a bowling alley. "You have four tries, in this particular game, to knock all the pins over. For best results, aim at Merlin," she suggested as an afterthought. "And here's the good part. Since we have no real bowls, we use… these!" And with a theatrical swoop of her arm to present the four pangolins, she cried, "Alarm!" At which the pangolins immediately turned into balls.

"Shazam!" Mercedes exclaimed to add drama to the act, because she thought all magicians tended to shout out something like that.

The captain was just about to pick up Pascal and roll him toward the ten pin meerkats, when there was a loud 'ping' sound. He took a small flat object out of his pocket and looked at it eagerly. "Hold it there," he said, "I have to go to my cabin. I'll be right back."

The cabin!

Now the animals were faced with a real alarm!

The line of command was alerted immediately. They had about a minute, to get Busby out, Archimedes reckoned.

CHAPTER 12

In the cabin, Busby had come across more photos of the captain posing with dead animals. Elephants mainly, but also gazelles and zebras. He was about to jump off the desk and take a look at a pile of screwed up paper in the waste paper basket under it, when he got another shock. There was a sudden pinging sound and the screen of the computer sprang to life right in front of his face.

Just three words appeared, in capital letters: IN-COMING ENCRYPTED MESSAGE.

Busby repeated the words to himself once or twice. It could be important.

As he hopped down to investigate the screwed up pieces of paper in the waste paper basket, he froze yet again. A key was turning in the cabin door lock! He hadn't heard a warning knock!

And for good reason; there hadn't been one!

There was no time to get to the port hole. The captain's feet were coming in through the door. What had gone wrong with the chain of command? Hugh again?

There was no point wondering about that now, Busby had to act quickly. All he could think to do was to jump up and cling to the bottom of the desk in the hope that the captain didn't look under it.

Busby wonders where to hide

And please, please, don't let him glance at the port hole. He would immediately spot the rope hanging there!

On deck, mission control couldn't understand why Busby hadn't tugged at the rope.

"This ain't good!" Chuck said, wondering what their next plan of action should be if Busby reappeared in the grip of the captain. "This sure ain't good," he re-emphasized.

Busby was hanging on like grim death. Suddenly, he thought he had been discovered. He found himself being pulled from under the desk! But he was still clinging desperately to the bottom of it. Then he realized. He must be hanging on to the bottom of a drawer. And now, directly in front of his nose, not an inch from it, was the captain's smelly belly button poking out from his overstretched shirt. Through all Busby's fears and thoughts of being found out, came the realization that had he opted for a peg on his nose, it would have been sticking into the captain's belly right now and all hell would be breaking out!

The shocks were never-ending. Now came some thunderous tapping from above, and the vibration of it nearly made Busby lose his grip. When that stopped, the sound of a printing machine nearly deafened him. And then came the coupe de grace, you might call it. The drawer was shoved so fiercely back to where it had started from that Busby couldn't hold on anymore. Fearing the worse, he prepared himself for a noisy fall and painful end to his masquerade. But another shock. This time though, it was a good one. Instead of hitting the cabin floor, he fell straight into the waste paper basket and was instantly covered by the screwed up balls of paper. Just a crack was left that he could see through with one eye. And then that itself was covered as the captain threw away his latest print-out, and with a double turn of the lock, was gone.

All the animals in the know had gathered around the top of the stairs leading from below expecting the worst. What could be done if their 'hero' had been discovered?

But he hadn't been!

The relief the conspirators felt when the captain reappeared single-handed, seemingly unperturbed, would have lifted a hot air balloon. They had all been holding their breath for such a long time.

"Right! Where were we?" he barked, making for his seat. Then thinking; 'Hmm. Why were they all waiting for me like that?'

As soon as the captain's footsteps had safely gone, Busby scrambled out of the basket clutching two of the discarded screwed up balls of paper. He didn't dare take more than two in case it was noticed they'd gone missing. He fluffed up what was left in the basket to make it look as if nothing had changed.

As he was about to jump up to the port hole, he noticed a large map of the world fixed to the wall underneath it. He hadn't seen it on his way in. In one of the vast blue bits, the oceans he guessed, there was a red pin marking a spot. "EXCHANGE POINT NOON DAY 9. LAT 5S. LON 45E.' Was scribbled beneath it.

'That's something else I really must remember.' Busby told himself as he slipped the loop under his arms and prepared to be hauled up. He tugged at the rope. And then he tugged again. There was no response! Where were they? It wasn't much of a joke if that's what they were playing.

With the swinging and the tugging and the whoosh of the sea flowing past, Busby lost the grip of one of the scrunched up pieces of paper.

And it dropped!

"Oh, no!" he cried aloud. He had already been feeling queasy just hanging there. But looking down at the bubbling waves to see where the ball of paper had gone made him feel really sick. What if the thing had fallen back inside the cabin?

It had! But it hadn't fallen onto the cabin floor. It had rested precariously on the catch that locked the porthole when it was pulled shut. It was fluttering dangerously and looked as though it might fall inside at any second.

Busby was swinging back and forth to the gentle motion of Pandora. Each time he swung near the port hole, he stretched out with one of his back paws and tried to grab the errant piece of paper. "Please don't make me have to go back in for it!" he begged.

On deck, Mercedes quickly lead the captain back to

the performance area, while, the other conspirators returned at a rate of knots to the top end of Busby's rope.

As the captain contemplated which of the rolled up pangolins to hurl at Merlin and the meerkat pins, Christopher looked over the side at the port hole. There he could see Busby swinging freely, so there was no need to wait for a tug on the rope.

What happened next would go down as the luckiest moment of the whole campaign.

In order to get to the fallen piece of paper, Busby had slipped out of the loop at the precise moment Christopher had stopped looking down. The little bush-baby was already clutching the other screwed up paper ball in one hand and didn't want to lose that. To keep his other hand free to grab what he needed, he wrapped his tail around the loop in the rope a few times. He really didn't want to lose that rope!

As he leaned in through the port hole, he felt his tail being pulled. "Ooherrrr!" he cried as he started to move upwards. He unwound his tail just enough to be able to stretch further down and, at the very last gasp, managed to seize the snagged paper ball in the nick of time before finding himself out of reach, being hauled up the side of the boat.

As he reached the top - tail first! - the looks on the faces of his awaiting friends told him they must have been having some shocks of their own while he

73

had been down below.

There were questioning looks all round, but relief soon took over. At first, Busby couldn't speak. He just waved his tiny clenched fists, wide-eyed, not only with the delayed realization of what he had just survived, but also in trepidation of what he was clutching in those tiny fists of his - not to mention what he had seen in the cabin.

CHAPTER 13

There was a mighty roar from the captain. The conspirators turned as one to obscure Busby as he jumped onto the deck and swiftly removed the evidence of the looped rope. But they need not have worried. The captain was celebrating scoring a strike, using Pascal as the bowl!

The meerkat pins who had been knocked over got to their feet and brushed themselves down. Pascal stopped being a ball and started nursing his bruises. He had been hurled so fiercely and rolled into Merlin with such force as to scatter most of the younger pins before he had even reached them. This idea of Mercedes had seemed alright on paper, but in the flesh, appropriate word, it wasn't much fun for the participants. Merlin was in full agreement with Pascal about this.

With the pins that had scattered, staying scattered, leaving only five to be aimed at, the game was abandoned.

Mr Pangolin whizzes toward Merlin's ten pin troupe

"Hah!" the captain bellowed. "Call these tricks? I need something spectacular. High wire sort of stuff! Don't any of you have talent?"

With that, to everyone's relief, he went below decks.

There was equal relief that Busby, the hero, had managed to survive his ordeal and had come out of it unscathed. But before he reported his findings, he wanted to know what had gone wrong with the chain of command. Why hadn't he been warned that the captain was coming back to the cabin?

"It was such a shock when I heard the key in the lock. I nearly did something in my pants!" he admitted. "Then there would have been a real mess!"

The conspirators all put their hands up guiltily. "What can we tell ya, Busby, buddy?" Chuck confessed apologetically. "We screwed up big time!" They had forgotten to replace Busby at the end of the command line. And since Busby was on the inside, he couldn't be the one doing the knocking on the door from the outside. "We owe you one, dude."

"Five," Busby argued to increase the conclave's embarrassment.

Chuck smiled at Busby's impertinence, or pertinence, actually, because he was right. All five of them had failed to spot their mistake. "OK, Buddy. Done deal. You got it! So what's the story down there?"

The five listened in silence in the seclusion of Chuck's lifeboat as the hero recalled everything in fine detail. He missed nothing.

The guns and photographs spoke for themselves.

"Trophy hunter!"

"Murderer!"

"The man has to be stopped!"

The Incoming Encrypted Message had come from an organisation calling themselves 'Offshore Trophy Traders'! OTT.

There could be little doubt what that meant!

The messages themselves were just a jumble of randomly mixed up letters. The code would have to be broken to make any sense of them, although that wasn't really necessary. They had already worked out what was in store for them. They had jumped out of the frying pan into the fire by coming on this fake 'holiday'.

But this didn't stop Archimedes from engrossing himself in the intriguing challenge of breaking that code. He was already on the case.

"Did you notice any books with jumbled up letters like the ones in these messages?" he asked Busby. "Might have had 'Codes' written on it?"

"No, nothing like that," Busby answered assuredly. "It's a fairly small cabin. I even looked under the bunk. Nothing there but an overflowing ash tray."

"That's good! That's very good!" Archimedes was plainly excited about this new challenge. "That sort of suggests the code could have quite a simple logic. Leave it with me."

The message written on the map under the circled red pin filled them all with foreboding. Exchange Point could only mean one thing.

"We're being dumped!"

"Exchanged?"

"Sold! For green backs!" Chuck was absolutely sure about this.

There were a few embarrassed glances over shoulders to see if anyone had a green back, until Archimedes put them straight. "You mean dollars?"

"You betcha! C.A.S.H." Chuck spelled the letters out. "It stands out a mile. I tell ya, dudes, even without breaking that code we gotta do something. No question!"

Anxious glances passed from one to the other. Noon. Day 9 was just beginning to sink in.

"Remind me," Chuck asked no-one in particular, already knowing the answer. "What day are we on?"

It was Day 7, and counting.

They needed to come up with something at once if they were to save themselves.

And it was Christopher who took the initiative. He had an idea and invited all able bodied adults to gather round to consider it.

Before he began, he asked Merlin and Mercedes if they wouldn't mind getting their children to keep watch on all the stairways to make sure the captain didn't suddenly come up and hear what was going on.

Mercedes nudged Merlin and he took off to muster

the young meerkats.

"I've been thinking a lot about this thing of the captain wanting really spectacular acts, "Christopher began confidentially. "Well, I think I've hit on one that might just do the trick, so to speak. A high wire act like no other!"

He set about describing his plan in great detail, then went over it again. By the third time he had gone through it, excitement was mounting. Those who had been assigned as helpers where repeating to themselves what they had to do. There must be no mistakes, no absent positions. Busby had endorsed this last point vigorously. It was potentially a very dangerous trick, so nothing should be out of place. And it was the danger in it that Christopher considered the captain would go for.

"Who says you're the stupid twin now?" Archimedes said, ruffling up his brother's red crop of hair affectionately. "Brilliant plan, Chris. And very brave! So, let's do it! First thing tomorrow morning. Day 8!"

The rest of the day saw dry runs of the performance. They had to be dry runs, because using the main prop might give the game away. To some of the animals not involved, especially Hugh and Hildegard, it seemed the monkeys and apes were practicing a sort of barn dance. They would stand in a circle then run in to the centre and high-five each other. Being very fit by now, Bono made sure all his troupe were central to the act.

While all that was going on, Archimedes battled with breaking the code encrypted in the print-outs. It would still be worth knowing what was in them, even though the plan of action had been set in motion and there could be no turning back.

"How's it going, Archie, my man?" Chuck asked, seeing him pawing over a bunch of letters he'd scribbled down. "Any closer to unraveling it?"

"Not as yet," Archimedes admitted. "I'm sure it's a pretty straight forward code. I'm working systematically through the simple ones."

"You reckon you'll break it?"

"You betcha!" Archimedes replied. He enjoyed stealing Chuck's expressions. "Gotta stop this knucklehead!"

"Hey, wise guy," Chuck said in jest. "You betcha? Knucklehead? Don't take advantage of a poor yank rodent. Get back to your QED business!"

"Gotcha!" came the response.

CHAPTER 14

That evening, there was a brilliant sunset, which played its part in calming the atmosphere on deck despite the urgency of the situation. Bunny and Monty, the Riverine rabbits, were staring at it as if caught in a car's headlights. Chuck joined them jauntily, seemingly more relaxed now that there was a plan in place to turn the tide.

"Hey guys, can I ask you something?" he said breezily. His curiosity had finally got the better of him. "How come you got named Bunny, Bunny. I mean, I thought, ya know, all rabbits were called 'bunny' rabbits. Know what I'm saying? What's the point of doubling up on it? And, ya know, don't get me wrong, but isn't Bunny a sought of girl's name? And Monty, I guess, would be a boy's?"

"We were wondering when someone might ask that," Monty answered with a single twitch of her nose, and a 'carry on' smile from Bunny. "They got us two mixed up when we were little, we were so much alike. So he's Bunny, and I'm Monty. There were quite a lot of us to start with, but…" She paused and Bunny quickly continued for her. "Yes, well, enough said. We were the last born and there were so many of us our parents ran out of names to call us, so they used short versions of our posh name Bunolagos Monticularis, which could also explain the 'bunny' tag that all rabbits get called. Anyway, What's in a name? We're happy."

"Well, what-do-ya-know!" Chuck exclaimed, blowing a long whistle. "I like your attitude, guys."

By now the sun had touched the horizon. All the animals were silently watching it in awe. They had never seen sunsets like these over the ocean before. Mountains and trees usually got in the way back home.

When it had completely disappeared, leaving a glorious glow in the sky,

Chuck lowered himself into his lifeboat, where Archimedes was still working on the encoded messages. With him to help were Mercedes, Pascal and Busby, whose big eyes in particular could see the letters better in the moonlight. They weren't going to bed just yet.

The first message was very short. The date suggested it was the last one that had been received, the one that had frightened Busby out of his wits when it burst onto the computer screen.

It was impossible to understand: ZGV BGILU GSTRV HIFLS GGL

… or pronounce!

The second was a much longer jumble, and it was this that gave Archimedes more hope.

There was something about it that he couldn't quite put his finger on.

It started with GMVNVVITZ.. What a tongue twister!

Then went on in what looked like five different segments, or paragraphs.

Totally unreadable.

Archimedes studied and studied each in turn.

"It's staring me in the face," he mumbled to his expectant friends. "What is it about this message that is telling me something?"

He seemed to go into a trance, deep in thought.

And then it came to him!

"Numbers!" he hissed like a wizard. "It's a list! A numbered list! And the numbers are written out in letters!"

It was a breakthrough, but it wasn't the end of it. There was still a lot of jiggling to be done.

But if he could fathom out how the numbers were coded, he would have cracked it!

For three hours Archimedes battled with some basic permutations. His trance-like state had returned and his friends knew not to disturb it.

Deep into the night, at last a possible solution came to him. There was a crafty twist to it, if he had got it right. By then, his assistants had all fallen asleep. He would join them for an hour or two in slumber, then wake them up at dawn to help him put his theory to the test.

Vernon had volunteered to keep Pandora on the straight and narrow course during the night. In the early hours of the morning, a bright full moon rose, bringing a shimmering reflection on the calm sea almost directly on the line he was steering. In its light, he saw something that immediately caught his attention, a disturbance that left a circle of little ripples radiating toward him. 'What's causing that?' he asked himself, wondering if he should change course to avoid whatever it was.

And then he got his answer.

Merlin was asleep, snuggled up with his arms around all his little ones. Vernon hopped down from the steering wheel to wake him. He wanted him to see this as well.

Coming with swishing sounds, shining silver in the moonlight, was sprouting a series of water fountains from a huge head which rose and dipped in the waves.

"What's going on? What's going on?" Merlin muttered in confusion as Vernon shook him awake

"Look! Look!" Vernon replied with glee. "It's Mr. Blue Whale!"

Merlin quickly woke his children. He didn't want them to miss this spectacular sight. They all gazed wide-eyed at the size of this massive creature.

"Ah!" the whale breathed with his big wide mouth. "I'm glad I've found someone awake on board at this

late hour. I have some important information perhaps you should know."

Vernon and Merlin looked at each other. Was this
going to be good news or bad news?

Mr. Blue Whale soon answered that question.

"Not far from here," he began, dipping down then
up again, "in the direction you seem to be heading,
my friends and I have spotted a large factory ship."
Down he dipped again, coming up to continue: "We
have seen this ship before, and it is not a nice ship.
We whales have kept well away from it because it
has hunted some of us down for its own evil pur-
poses. What's more, we don't think we're the only
creatures it is trying to capture. There are many
large cages on its decks!"

Vernon and Merlin exchanged glances again. One of
them should explain.

 It was Merlin. "Funny you should tell us that. Well,
not funny, actually." he went on to explain what the
animals had discovered about the captain's intentions, and the plan that Christopher had come up
with that it was hoped would save them.

"Bravo, Christopher, is all I can say," the whale
spurted out. "Well, we whales and dolphins have
been planning something too. Something that
could be a benefit to us all."

At that point, Mrs. Blue Whale popped her head up
and spoke. "I don't know if you realised it, but Pan-

dora is going round in circles. Just thought I'd mention it."

With all the chat, Vernon had neglected the steering wheel.

He rushed up to it and put Pandora quickly back onto the correct compass heading just as the captain came storming onto deck brandishing one of his hunting guns.

"What's going on?" he yelled, going straight to Vernon at the helm. "It felt like we were changing direction."

Vernon gave a nonchalant shrug as if to say 'Don't know what you're talking about' and the captain calmed down. "H'm," he muttered, slapping the butt of his rifle as if to make a point. "Just be sure to keep this old crate on line!"

He strolled around the deck for a while, from time to time jerking the gun to his shoulder and pointing it at nothing in particular as if testing his reflexes. "Not long now," he could be heard muttering to himself as he went below decks.

With him gone, Mr. Whale put his head up again and said: "I can see exactly why you have to do something about that man. He's just like the ones on that factory ship I've told you about." With a final spout from his blow-hole, he added: "We'll be off now to get on with our own plan. But, trust us, we'll be close by if you need us."

CHAPTER 15

After the whales had gone, Merlin couldn't get back to sleep. He knew he had to tell the gang what had happened, so at first light he went to Chuck's lifeboat to wake them.

Archimedes was already awake, aching to test his theory about the code. With this fresh news from the whales, he was even more anxious to get on with it. He rallied his sleeping friends and told them Merlin's news before anxiously getting back to his code-breaking.

"To test it, we need some dust and a safe place. Let's find somewhere flat near Mr. Elephant. That should do it."

Busby, Pascal, Mercedes and Chuck, were roused by Archimedes' enthusiasm, but didn't quite understand his demands.

They went to wake Mr. Elephant and Archimedes explained what was happening. From a bag of dust that had been swept up the day before, a thin layer was spread on the deck. As he called letters out, Archimedes wanted someone to scratch them into it. "This is where Mr. Elephant comes into the equation," Archimedes couldn't resist taking the opportunity to use that word. It was Mr. Elephant's job to blow away the evidence with his trunk should the captain suddenly appear on deck for some unforeseen reason.

Archimedes gathered his thoughts for a moment. Then, studying the short print-out message in front of him, he asked Busby to write the letter A. Next it was a T. Then came E.

"Make a space now, Busby."

Busby obliged.

"Right, the second word," Archimedes announced. So the first word was ATE, which everyone thought was curious. But the next words were even curiouser, as someone had once said incorrectly. YTROF, THGIE, SRUOH, and finally, TTO.

Archimedes had such a thrilled expression on his face, anticipation mounted in all around him

"My word," Mr. Elephant exclaimed, quite appropriately. "I think he's got it!"

"Got it?" Chuck queried, questionably. He wasn't so sure. Apart from the word ATE, the rest were just as gobbledygook as the ones written on the print-out.

"Yes! Got it!" Archimedes confirmed in celebration. He could hardly contain his elation. "Don't you see? It was the double twist that confused me."

They didn't. But he went on to enlighten them.

"If you twist the words round," he revealed, literally jumping up and down on the spot. "They read: ETA FORTY EIGHT HOURS. OTT."

He had to determine the first twist, first, of course. The break through came when he realized there were numbers in the message, written out as letters, not numbers like 1, 2, 3, 4, 5.

ONE was written VML, TWO was LDG, then came THREE, VVISG, which was the biggest clue. I suddenly saw that the E's were V's, the T's, G's and the O's, L's. The numbers were written backwards! It was the double twist that kept leading me astray. It came to me in my dreams. The alphabet was turned on itself so that A=Z, B=Y, C=X and so on," he clarified, then added for fun. "QED! Which would have been coded as WVJ."

The amazement of those paying attention was suddenly brought to a halt.

The very acute ears of Busby had detected movement on the stairs.

"Alarm!" he hissed, all but turning Pascal into a ball as Mr. Elephant, with one swift blow of his trunk, sent the dust flying and with it the decoded message.

But there had been no need to panic. It was Christopher, not the captain, coming up from below with some of the helpers needed for his daring performance. He wanted to have an early run through to keep everyone on their toes. Among them were the colourful Mandrills, who had suspected from the start that things were not quite right about this cruise. They were only too pleased now to be in cahoots with Christopher and his inspired rescue act. They stood like warriors at is side.

Mr Elephant quickly explained what Archimedes had achieved, stressing the urgency of their situation.

The 'ETA' in the message was short for estimated time of arrival, and that message had come 12 hours ago. So the 48 hours was now 36! Day 9! Only a day and a half to the exchange point! Which, as was explained by Archimedes, was pin-pointed by the 'LAT 5 S LON 45 E' Busby had seen written on the map. Latitude 5 degrees South (of the equator) Longitude 45 degrees East (of the Greenwich Meridian). Nowadays, satellites encircling the planet worked this out in milliseconds, which was crucial for airplanes and ocean liner, and also sometimes when drivers lose their way in a car. But, right now, for Pandora and her 'special cargo', knowing their exact position wasn't going to change their situation at all.

At breakfast, while the captain was making his count, Diana, the little dik dik, who had been chosen to approach him told him about the spectacular trick that was being planned for him. It would be nothing like the silly games of yesterday, but a real circus trick that even needed a safety net. It was so dangerous and awe-inspiring.

She had been told to make it sound as unmissable as possible, and she had done a good job.

'If it needs a safety net, this might well be what I'm looking for,' the captain told himself. "And who will be performing this amazing trick?" he asked.

"Christopher, sir," Diana told him, trying to make it sound even more exciting. "Although it is a very dangerous trick, we have all agreed to let him to do it, knowing how much you want to see a really ground-breaking circus trick. Shall I tell him to get ready, sir?"

"Yes, please do. It sounds exactly what I need." the captain responded with a politeness not known of him before. This dik dik has got the right attitude, he was thinking. Perhaps she could be worked into this act, if it's as exciting as it sounds it might be.

Diana had been laying on the charm like a true professional. 'She'd do well in show business given half a chance,' Mercedes was thinking.

With breakfast over, what there was of it, word spread fast among the creatures who still thought they were on a holiday cruise that something important was about to happen.

They were all gathered up around Chuck's lifeboat to hear more about it.

Chuck stood up with Archimedes at his side. "Ok guys, listen up, and listen up good, especially the ones who still think that this is a holiday cruise. Archimedes has got to the bottom of something we've kept from most of you for reasons of security. And for that reason again, we don't want no screeching or squealing when you hear what he's gonna tell ya. So cover your juniors' ears or take 'em some place else for a bit. Over to you, Archie, buddy."

With appropriate ceremony, Archimedes, surveyed the silent crowd before him. "This is a message sent to the captain three days ago that I finally managed to decode," he pronounced, "It is in the form of an agreement that he made with an offshore animal trafficking company. OTT. There are five clauses to it. And it was the numbering of the clauses that gave me the breakthrough."

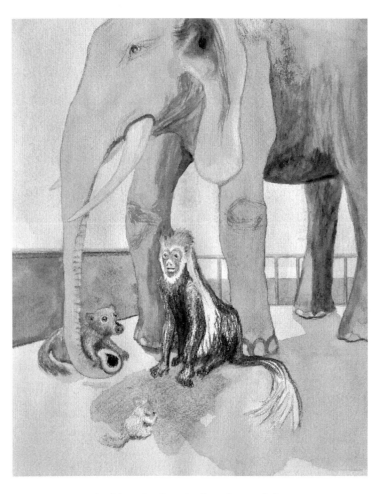

Archimedes has broken the code!

Taking a deep breath, he began reading the clauses out with due solemnity.

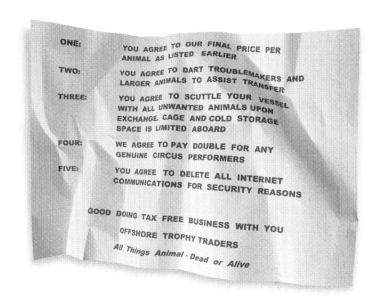

ONE: YOU AGREE TO OUR FINAL PRICE PER ANIMAL AS LISTED EARLIER

TWO: YOU AGREE TO DART TROUBLEMAKERS AND LARGER ANIMALS TO ASSIST TRANSFER

THREE: YOU AGREE TO SCUTTLE YOUR VESSEL WITH ALL UNWANTED ANIMALS UPON EXCHANGE. CAGE AND COLD STORAGE SPACE IS LIMITED ABOARD

FOUR: WE AGREE TO PAY DOUBLE FOR ANY GENUINE CIRCUS PERFORMERS

FIVE: YOU AGREE TO DELETE ALL INTERNET COMMUNICATIONS FOR SECURITY REASONS

GOOD DOING TAX FREE BUSINESS WITH YOU

OFFSHORE TROPHY TRADERS

All Things Animal - Dead or Alive

He chose not to read out the last three words – DEAD OR ALIVE!

Even without them, tears started flowing uncontrollably.

"Cages! My little ones wouldn't be able cope!" Mercedes declared, terrified at the thought.

"Us big ones, either," Mr. Rhinoceros pointed out.

Unwanted! Cold Storage! Scuttled! They didn't need to hear 'dead or alive'.

"Okay, okay," Chuck tried to calm them. "Kinda hard to take, ain't it? But something's being done to get us out of this. That's why Chris came up with this trick he's gonna perform. And it comes with a great twist, you betcha! We had to break this bad news to you before he does it, just so's all of you've got a handle on why we're gonna do what we're gonna do. Everyone's gotta play along so the evil Sap doesn't catch on. So big smiles all round, okay?" With that he slipped out of sight into his lifeboat. It was too soon to be seen by the captain. It might put a spanner in the works.

Tears were wiped away amid nervous mutterings. The Riverine rabbits were quick to teach some of the little ones how to do fake smiles, like the ones that came naturally to them.

"We must all be patient for the time being," Mr. Elephant advised, now feeling calmer. "The captain must not get the slightest hint that we have found out about his wickedness and lies. And let no-one be alarmed by what you are going to see when Christopher does his trick. It could free us all."

If an elephant could cross his fingers, that's what Mr. Elephant would have been doing right now.

The preparations began.

CHAPTER 16

One of Pandora's loading nets was to act as a safety net. Christopher asked Charlie, a rather keen chimpanzee to go down and hook it onto the crane.

"Aye, aye, captain," Charlie responded with a salute, and then corrected himself. "I meant to say, aye, aye, Christopher, but the words slipped..." He stopped for fear of digging a bigger hole for himself, having called Christopher 'captain'. The real captain had been listening.

"And don't steal any bananas while you're down there." that captain snapped.

Charlie hadn't thought of that. There were still a few bananas in the hold. One might not be missed. But no, it wouldn't be fair. Right now, anyway. One for all, all for one!

With the hook connected, he shouted up from the hold, "Haul away, me mateys! Job done." He clung to the net fancying himself as a real sailor as Pandora's crane hauled him all the way up to the deck.

Once there, the net was lowered to where Christopher wanted it, at which, Charlie jumped off niftily and unhooked it, spreading it out flat as requested for the upcoming performance.

The hook was handed to Charlie's wife, Charmaine. She had been well rehearsed in what to do with it when beckoned.

With everything in place, Christopher climbed up to the top of the crane and carefully moved out to the very end of it. "Safety net in position, please, directly beneath me" he shouted down. "I am about to perform the most amazing trick you will ever see, and I am sure you will all be extremely impressed." Well, perhaps all but one of you, he thought to himself. "I will leap from this very great height, down onto the safety net, and when I bounce up, as if on a trampoline, I shall perform an extraordinary vault that will out-do anything ever seen at the Olympic Games.

'That would be a Yurchenko half-on front layout with a twist,' thought Imogen, an impala who knew all about leaps and vaults, being pretty good at them herself. 'If he matches that, I will be very impressed indeed. Never seen one done properly.'

"It is called," Christopher continued, in no great hurry. He wanted to build up the tension and anticipation. But while he paused, he forgot the name of the vault he was supposed to be doing. "Perhaps Archimedes could take it from here," he called down hopefully, "while I prepare myself?"

Archimedes could see that his brother was in trouble by the look on his face, even from his great height. "Indeed, my brave brother," he said proudly. "This stunning, if not to say, amazing trick that many gymnasts will not dare to attempt is, as Diana our lovely dik dik has mentioned, truly ground-breaking, or, in this case, especially if no safety net was available, truly deck-breaking. It is called a Yurchenko full-on front to back layout with a double twist!"

"Well I never! A full double double!" Imogen gasped with such astonishment that all around her gasped as well. "I didn't know one like that even existed."

It didn't. Archimedes was just improvising.

"But I stress," Christopher wanted to point out, having remembered his lines, "that everyone must watch very carefully, so as not to miss the double twist at the end. That is the most exciting part. Also, please note, the trick will happen so quickly, that if you blink, you might even miss the full lay-out Yurchenko bit as well."

The captain was getting impatient with all these preparations, but he sensed that at last he might be getting a performance that would impress the OTT people enough to pay him properly. He felt he deserved it, with all he'd had to go through to get the animals this far.

He didn't know it, but this performance was designed to give him exactly what he deserved.

Christopher was about to cue the elephants to trumpet a fanfare, when something caught his eye. From his great height he could see a lot of fountains spouting around Pandora. He felt most honoured. Not only was he to have a fanfare, but also a water display from Mr. Whale, and his friends.

Christopher raised both arms, and called down: "Safety net up, please. Nice and tight, to give me enough bounce to perform the biggest twist you'll ever see."

"Hup, one, two, pull!" Bono urged, prompting Vernon, Charlie, Merlin, the mandrills and the whole team of his able-bodied apes and monkeys to take up positions. They all knew exactly what to do. Holding the outer edges of the net, they stretched it as tightly as they could.

"For those interested," Archimedes pointed out. "An insight into Einstein's theory of relativity will be demonstrated in Christopher's leap." This was quite an unrehearsed diversion from planned proceedings, and no-one was at all interested, or could even understand what Archimedes was going on about. But he wouldn't be stopped. "Christopher will land in the net in a seemingly perpendicular descent relative to his release point on the crane," he went on regardless. "Now, since Pandora is moving in the water, shall we say at eight feet per second and the fall takes two seconds, Christopher would land 2 x 8 feet further forward into the sea if Pandora and the net were suddenly not there to catch him. QED. But since Christopher can't swim, it's just as well Pandora can't get out of the way in two seconds."

With that brief and not particularly wanted complication over, attention went back to Christopher.

"Fanfare now, please," Archimedes prompted the elephants. "I think this is it!"

From behind the captain, a loud harmonious chord was trumpeted, the baby trunk hitting the highest note, which triggered a cascade of fountains around Pandora.

With this curtain-raising fanfare of water music, the scene was set. Christopher, with his arms raised, began his count.

The captain looked up in eager anticipation.

"One.......two.......three......!"

Upon the count of 'three', Christopher leapt off the crane in a spectacular dive, curling himself into a ball as he came down. He landed just as Archimedes had predicted, directly in the centre of the outstretched net and immediately bounced up again. As he went up, he unfolded himself and prepared for the great double twist.

And what a twist it was!

But it wasn't Christopher doing it!

At his highest point, he grabbed an overhanging rope that had been placed there for that purpose and looked down in time to see Mr. Elephant tuck his tusks under the captain's armpits and throw him into the net.

As soon as he landed, Bono cried, "Hup! Hup!" and everyone holding tightly to the net ran in as if doing the barn dance they had been rehearsing and bundled the captain up in it, tying the ends with a double twist.

"Hook!" Christopher now shouted and Charmaine came running forward with the hook.

Within seconds of Christopher's bounce, the net had been hoisted high above the deck with the captain safely bound up in it.

"What a trick!" all were shouting with glee.

"Bravo!" they cheered and chanted, "Marvellous! Wonderful! Magnificent! Three cheers for Christopher!"

"A twist to end all twists!" Imogen had to admit, "Even without the slightest hint of a Yurchenko."

"Now you see why it's called a 'safety net'!" Archimedes couldn't resist declaring. "The captain is safely secured in it and his wicked dealings will be exposed! What's more, we all have our freedom again, even if some of us didn't know we had nearly lost it in the first place."

"Let me down this minute!" the captain was pleading to no avail, "This is no joke!"

And it wasn't a joke, all agreed. No joke whatsoever. This was really happening.

Christopher swung down as Chuck appeared from his hide out. The high five four and a half ganged up slapping each other on the back, high fiving again and again with anyone available.

"What a team!"

"You betcha!"

The captain's groans were beginning to annoy the animals. Let's take that Sap to the very highest point the crane will go?" Chuck suggested.

Up it went, all the time his cries getting quieter and quieter until they could hardly be heard at all.

That's better," all agreed.

CHAPTER 17

Attention now turned to the spectacular display of fountains surrounding Pandora.

"It's Mr. Blue Whale," the young meerkats cried. "Give us a shower, give us a shower!" They called out, and much to their delight, he did.

"Congratulations all aboard!" he cried. "Now, do you want the good news or the good news!" he spurted out.

"The good news! The good news!" came a chorus from the decks.

"Well, my friends, the first bit of good news is that we whales have teamed up with dozens of dolphins and we have found the freighter operating as OTT at your exchange point. It is indeed the factory ship I warned you about yesterday."

"And that's good news?" more than one animal gulped.

"Let me finish. Well, in case you didn't know it, dolphins are very nifty and clever creatures. And, with the help of us whales, they have succeeded in making this OTT organisation totally powerless. It can't move! It can only drift. And how has this been achieved, you wonder? By wrapping its propellers tightly in some of the huge piles of plastic we have been gathering up. The plastic has made the propellers seize up, which in turn has burnt out the engines! As our friend Chuck might say; 'The factory ship ain't going nowhere!' An appreciative nod from Chuck was accompanied by cheers and laughter. "So," the whale went on, "You've stopped the captain, and we've stopped OTT!" The other good news is that my friends and I have found an island where there are no homo sapiens. There are lots and lots of fruit and berry bushes. If you should want to, you could have a proper holiday there. It's got lovely beaches to play on and trees to swing in."

"Mr. whale has found an island!" the young meerkats cried out excitedly. "We can have a beach holiday now instead of being dragged around boring old buildings. Yippee!" Bright smiles spread like wild fire across Pandora's decks.

"Yes, you'll be able to have a whale of a time!" Mr. Whale joked.

However, the conclave of plotters pointed out that certain things had to be dealt with before holiday time could be declared: what was to be done with the captain and OTT. They had to be brought to justice!

But how to do it?

Archimedes volunteered his services.

He had always wanted to get his hands on a computer.

The cabin door keys were needed to allow this,

which were presumably in the captain's pocket and getting them might take a little while to achieve. However, the way they did it was a lot of fun. The captain was bounced rigorously up and down at the end of the crane until the keys dropped out!

It was Mercedes who outstretched the scramble to catch them. "How's that!" she cried as she lead the charge to the cabin. "And no steering 20 degrees off course while we're down there." she added grinning at Merlin, who had taken over the wheel.

The computer was already humming when they piled into the cabin. The first thing the animals did was to throw the guns out of the port hole with the boxes of ammunition, their evil use done with.

"Right," Archimedes started, looking at a screen with a lot of symbols on it. He clicked on one called 'Giggle'. He'd heard somewhere that this one could tell you almost anything.

"What shall I ask for?" he put to the gang.

"What about 'wildlife concern'?" Chuck suggested.

Archimedes tapped it in and 'Boom!' a whole world of help opened up.

Pages and pages devoted to animal concern!

"Wow!" Chuck cried. "How about that? Just take your pick, Archie boy!"

Archimedes liked the one with a little Panda as a mascot, WWF. World Wild Life it stood for.

A quick look at WWF's credentials told the gang they need go no further. If they passed on the details of their situation, including all the encrypted messages with an explanation of the code, OTT's evil trade would be exposed. The last thing he did was pass on 'LAT 5S LON 45E'. All this laboriously done, a response came back almost immediately. "Well done, Pandora's crew," it started. "We have been searching for this OTT vessel for some time. Thank you for the co-ordinates! At last we can arrange for our Marine Branch to impound it and arrest the culprits. Stay safe!"

Hi fives, and a few four and a halves went round the cabin. Life was getting better by the second.

The gang went to join the rest of the animals on the upper deck to relay the news. They had dealt with the fate of OTT. But what of the captain?

Mr. Whale had the answer.

"Before I take you to your holiday island, keep going until you get close to the burnt out OTT ship. Then simply throw the captain into the sea and let him swim for it.!"

"You got it, my friend!" Chuck rejoiced at the idea.

By first light the next morning, the factory ship came into view.

Every last one of the animals was awake and on deck not to miss the final act of their fake European Cruise.

And what fun it was to see the captain dropped wailing from Pandora's swinging crane into the ocean. He tried to shake a fist but nearly sank, so thought better of it.

With the captain at last gone, a sense of euphoria overtook all aboard.

Mr. Whale added to this by announcing that it was now time to turn Pandora round and follow him to their new holiday destination, the desert island.

"Hold on to the kids, Mercedes!" Merlin shouted (for a change) as he took Pandora into a sharp U-turn. Just as well, because the turn was so sharp, everyone had to hang on tightly.

Even Hugh and Hildegard were very happy now to have been mistaken about the captain's true intentions. A beach holiday on a desert island sounded much more romantic for a honeymoon than city tours, especially since it wasn't really a desert island, just deserted.

The blue whale and his friends formed a guard of honour for Merlin as he steered Pandora. It stretched far into the distance like a wide avenue lined with trees either side, except instead of trees there were fountains.

Pandora glided merrily along on the crest of a wave, or, rather, on the crests of several waves thrown up by the boulevard of whales and their huge swishing tails.

Early next day, Pandora had reached the deserted island and was safely anchored in a beautiful bay close to a crescent shaped beach. The animals were jubilantly happy. How wonderful their turnaround holiday was going to be!

As the wake of all the magnificently flapping tails disappeared, the animals got on with enjoying their new found freedom. "Hup, one, two, stretch," Bono soon had his team running up and down the beach, occasionally leading them into the sea to cool down.

Hugh and Hildegard pranced along the shallow waves occasionally splashing each other for fun and eventually came to rest on an outcrop of rocks at the end of the crescent shaped beach. They found a place to sit and gazed at the wonderful view.

"Really glad I brought my sun-glasses now," Hugh told Hildegard. "You can borrow them if you like." She declined.

Already on the rock, the Riverine rabbits were sun bathing, now with real smiles even bigger than Cheshire cats. At the highest point of the rock stood Mercedes, with Merlin and the young meerkats spread out around her, all looking out to sea again as if by habit.

Pip and Petra found a perfectly sheltered cave to base themselves. It wouldn't be long before the two of them would become three, so they needed some-where suitably spacious and secluded for the big event.

Archimedes had soon started a long trek around the perimeter of the island with great purpose, counting his steps. Then he was going to criss-cross it a few times in different directions to calculate its size. He was keen to discover if it was large enough to sustain their numbers for longer than just a holiday.

Most of the larger animals went directly to explore the interior of the island to see what it offered, with exactly the same thought in their heads.

While Harry went off to find a suitable site to dig a burrow for Hyacinth and the family, Nosy asked, "Do any of those 'why' berries grow here, mummy?"

The End

AFTERWORD

As a cameraman and documentary film maker, the   author has witnessed first hand the problems the   animals talk about in Pandora's Stowaway; the hunting, the poaching, the trapping, the destruction of habitat.

He has also experienced the good being done by groups on the African continent to protect the interests of   endangered species and the environment in the face of dwindling rain forests.

Printed in Great Britain
by Amazon

58642200R00069